THAT PERSON
IS NOT
IN THESE
COMICS

CONTENTS

THE PORTAL
STATION
2

TEAM PUGH SAVE
THE WORLD

BEFORE
NBA APOCOLYPSE

I THINK
WE'RE ALONE
NOW!

VILLAINS
MEDDLING
MOTHER

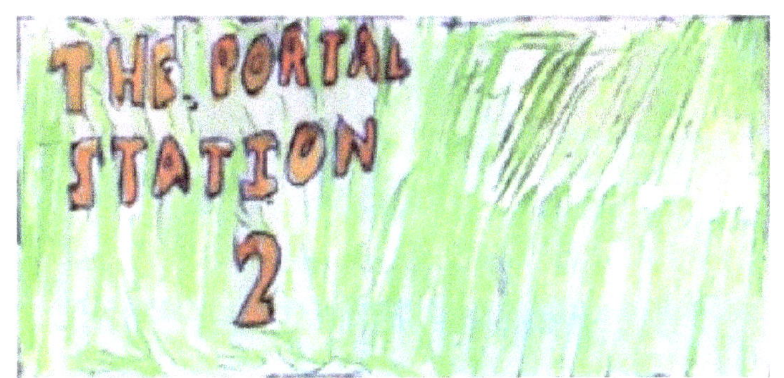

THE PORTAL
STATION
2

WIBBLE WOBBLE
WIBBLE WOBBLE

WIBBLE WOBBLE
WIBBLE WOBBLE

MACK AND TWO TEAM PUGH GRUNTS APPEARED IN PENTRAL COLLEGE IN THE FAR DISTANT FUTURE THEIR TIME MACHINE APPEARED IN THE AIR WITH A....

MACK REMEMBERED HIS CHILDHOOD BEST FRIEND MASON TIME TRAVELLED HERE FROM 2015

A CRONAL LINK! FROM 2022! I AM A DESCENDANT OF LYN LCOMBER 2015

THIS ENTIRE FUTURE TIMELINE IS FALLING APART! YOU HAVE TO GET UP THERE!
TELEPORT EARTH DATA THROUGH A DUP-TUNNEL!

WOOM!
YOU HAVE 30 SEC—
SHE VANISHED!

I KNOW WHAT I MUST DO!
?
30 SECONDS!?

AAAAAHHHHHHHHHH
!!!!
SPAWNING......DECO
OOOOOY!
AAAAAAAAAAAAAAA
AAAAAAAAAAAAAAA
AAAAAAAAAAAAAAA
AAAAAAAAAAAAAAA
AHHHHHHHHHHHHHH
HHHHHHHHHHHHHHHH
HHHHHHHHHHHHHHHH
HHH!!!!!!!!!!!!!!!!!!!
!!!!!!!!!!!!!!!!

EARTH IN 2022
WAS THEN SAVED
ZAP
A DUPLICATE APPEARED AS A DECOY
WILE THE ORIGINAL EARTH WAS SENT
2 DAYS INTO THE FUTURE THROUGH A
GIANT GREEN PORTAL!!!!

BUT MACK NOTICED
SOMEONE! HE COULD SEE
ALL THINGS BUT ONLY ONE
PERSON CAUGHT HIS EYE!
!!?
TO BE CONTINUED

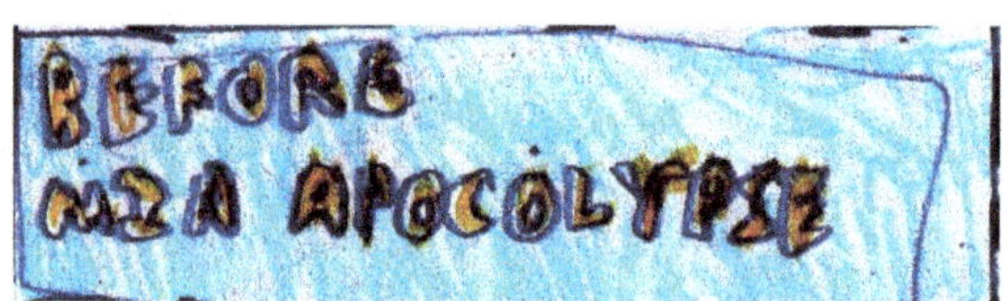

BEFORE
MIA APOCOLYPSE

THIS IS A HOUSE IN THE UK
BREAKING NEWS: LOCATION OF MIA MULLER STILL UNKNOWN
ALL WE DO KNOW IS....HOW BEAUTIFUL SHE IS

MEANWHILE IN A HOUSE IN PORT WHELLER – NJ – U.S.A (ONE MONTH EARLIER)

UNCLE, YOU ARE LOSER! WE ON THIS PLANET AND YOU NOT HAVE JOB
I GET MIA A JOB!

HE NOT KNOW HOW TO GET JOB COUSIN
I SHOW YOU
UM, MY DAD MIGHT BE SAD
CAN YOU APOLOGISE?
NO
WELCOME
CREEK
UM, I THINK I TRY JOB NORMAL WAY
WHAT YOU UP TO?

HERE I KEEP SOME GALACTIC OBJECTS IN HERE FROM FORBIDDEN TIMELINES
IT WHAT YOU NEED
PASS CAREFULLY
SO THIS FROM FORBIDEN TIMELINE?
YEAH IT'S MAGIC, IT'LL MAKE EVERYONE OBSESSED WITH YOU

OKAY NO ONE BE HURT BY US IF WE USE UP HERE
NOW PUT LIPSTICK ON THEN POST ON LINK'D IN THEN YOU GET MANY JOB OFFERS

YOU SURE THIS MAGIC LIPSTICK IS SAFE?
THE STORY CONTINUES IN "WILL YOU LIKE THESE COMICS?" BY OCEAN VERTES

I THINK WE'RE ALONE NOW!

A NIGHTMARE

SOMETHING WAS AT THE BOTTOM OF THE CORRIDOR!!!!

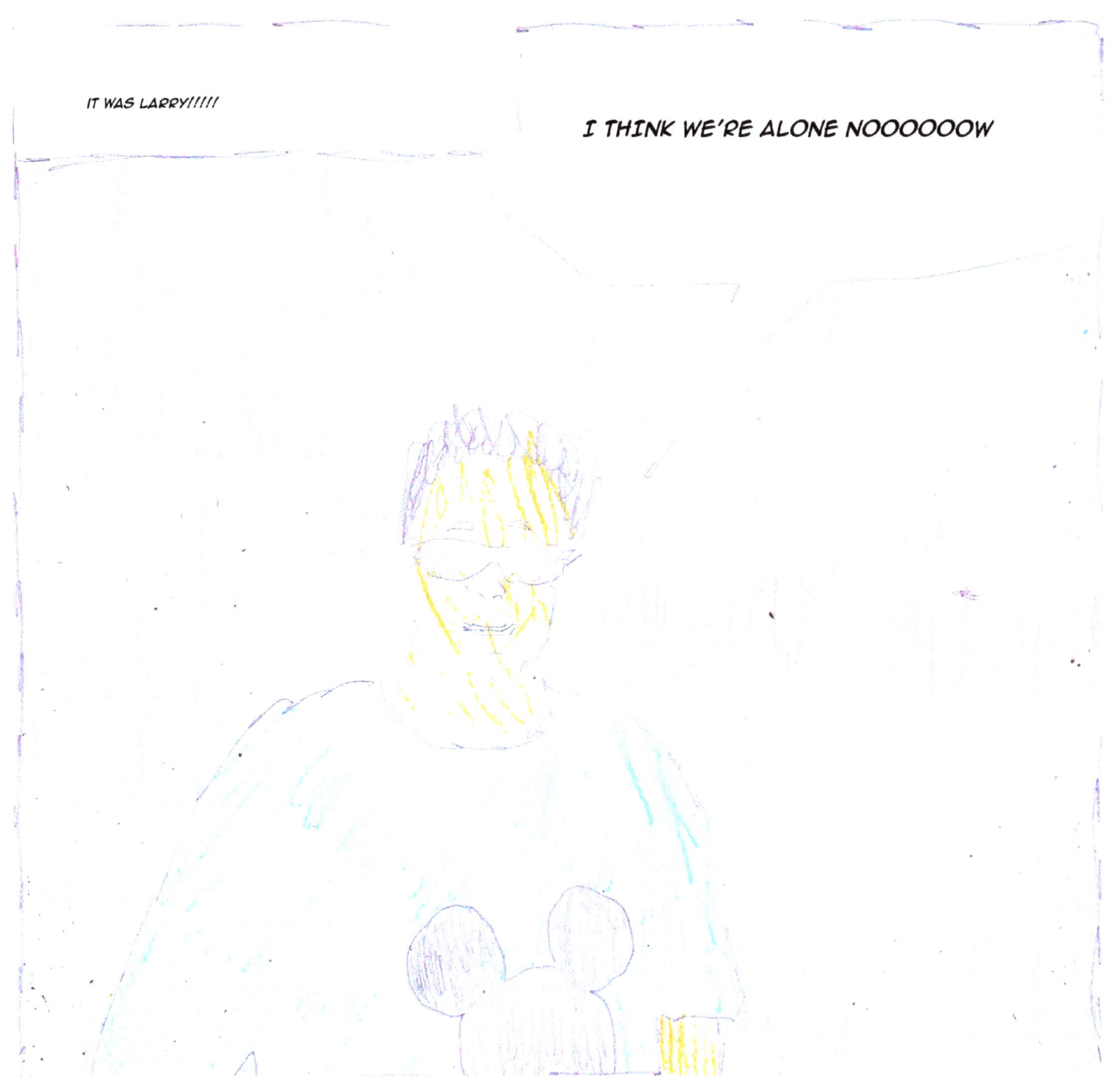

IT WAS LARRY!!!!!
I THINK WE'RE ALONE NOOOOOOW

GASP!

ARE YOU OKAY?
WHAT DO YOU KEEP
HAVING
NIGHTMARES
ABOUT?

SHE TURNED TO FIND HER NEW HUSBAND STANDING BY THE BED

THEM
NIGHTS

THANKS FOR
COMING DOWN
HERE LEXI

I'M ALWAYS HERE
WHEN YOU NEED TO
TALK, SO TELL ME,
WHAT'S GOING ON?

I JUST, I DON'T KNOW WHO I'VE MARRIED. WHEN WE FIRST MET HE, SEEMED ALRIGHT BUT HE'S JUST DIFFERENT, IT'S LIKE HE'S COMPLETELY LOST HIS MIND, HE PACES UP AND DOWN THE GARDEN JUGGLING A PINECONE, HE PUTS UP THESE FLAGS IN THESE RANDOM PLACES AND CALLS THEM L-SPOTS AND HE NEVER DID ANYTHING LIKE THAT BEFORE WE WERE MARRIED
I HAVE NIGHTMARES ABOUT HIM EVERY NIGHT...

WOW, OKAY.....SO

WHY HELLO DARLING

I GUESS YOU COULD SAY I COULDN'T BEAR TO SEE YOU LEAVE

FUNNY STORY I ENDED UP HAVING TO SMASH A PORTAL BECAUSE
KELSEA'S BOYFRIEND WENT ON TO RENT-A-GREEN-ARMOURED-
GUARD.COM AND LOTS OF THEM JUST START TELEPORTING AROUND
HER WHEREVER SHE WENT, BUT I TOOK THEM OUT THEN SMASH THE
PORTAL THEN FOUND THIS DREAM POD, I CAN GO INTO YOUR DREAM
AND FIGHT WHATEVER IT IS YOU KEEP HAVING NIGHTMARES ABOUT

VILLAINS
MEDDLING
MOTHER

DON'T USE THAT WORD
I DON'T LIKE THAT WORD

MOTHER,
PLEASE, THERE
IS NOTHING
WRONG WITH THE
WORD EVIL

I'M VERY DISAPPOINTED IN YOU
SON, YOU ARE HAVING NO
SUPPER FOR A WEEK

MOTHER, I AM A 61 YEAR OLD MAN....NOW , THE PLAN IS ABOUT TO TAKE ACTION!

TO BE CONTINUED

CONTACT INFO OCEANVERTES@GMAIL.COM